## Asterix the Legionary

Gaul was divided into three parts.
No, four parts — for one small village of
indomitable Gauls still held out against the
Roman invaders ...

Asterix and Obelix join a Roman legion — but
their ideas of military conduct are not quite
Roman. Strong men quail as this indomitable
couple do things their own way, and of
course succeed in their aim, the rescue of
the hero Tragicomix.

Also available in Knight

TEXT BY GOSCINNY

# Asterix the Legionary

DRAWINGS BY UDERZO

*Translated by Anthea Bell and*

*Derek Hockridge*

 **KNIGHT**

*The paperback division of Brockhampton Press*

ISBN 0 340 17656 3

This edition published 1973 by Knight, the paperback
division of Brockhampton Press, Leicester.
First published in 1970 by Brockhampton Press Ltd

Printed and bound in Great Britain
by Richard Clay (The Chaucer Press) Ltd
Bungay, Suffolk

The year is 50 BC. Gaul is entirely occupied
by the Romans. Well, not entirely...
One small village of indomitable Gauls still
holds out against the invaders. And life is not easy for the
Roman legionaries who garrison the fortified camps of
Totorum, Aquarium, Laudanum and Compendium...

Now turn the book sideways
and read on...

# a few of the Gauls

Asterix, the hero of these adventures. A shrewd, cunning little warrior; all perilous missions are immediately entrusted to him. Asterix gets his superhuman strength from the magic potion brewed by the druid Getafix...

Obelix, Asterix's inseparable friend. A menhir delivery-man by trade; addicted to wild boar. Obelix is always ready to drop everything and go off on a new adventure with Asterix—so long as there's wild boar to eat, and plenty of fighting.

Getafix, the venerable village druid. Gathers mistletoe and brews magic potions. His speciality is the potion which gives the drinker superhuman strength. But Getafix also has other recipes up his sleeve...

Finally, Vitalstatistix, the chief of the tribe. Majestic, brave and hot-tempered, the old warrior is respected by his men and feared by his enemies. Vitalstatistix himself has only one fear; he is afraid the sky may fall on his head tomorrow. But as he always says, "Tomorrow never comes."

Cacofonix, the bard. Opinion is divided as to his musical gifts. Cacofonix thinks he's a genius. Everyone else thinks he's un-speakable. But so long as he doesn't speak, let alone sing, everybody likes him....

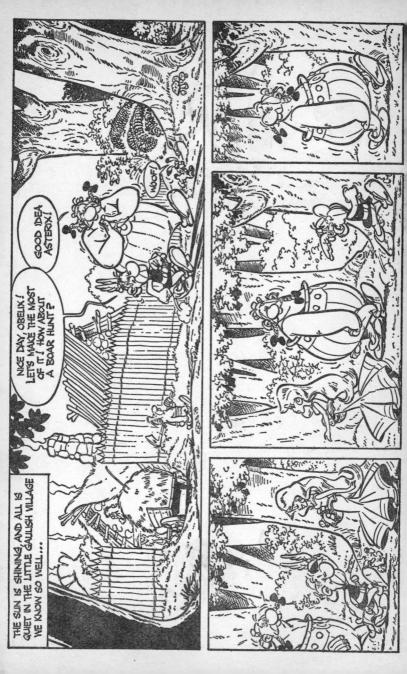

ENJOYING YOURSELF, OBELIX, PUSHING TREES OVER WHILE I'M UP IN THEM CUTTING MISTLETOE?

RIGHT! ARE WE GOING ON THIS HUNT?

BOOM! CRAAASH!

OUCH!

WELL...ER...WELL, IT'S AN UNTIDY SORT OF FOREST ANYWAY. TREES ALL OVER THE PLACE!

SEVERAL MINUTES LATER...

WE ONLY NEEDED TO STOP THEM!

WELL, WE HAVE STOPPED THEM!

OBELIX! WAIT A MINUTE!

RIGHT!

AVE...

POLITENESS WILL GET YOU EVERYWHERE, OBELIX...

WOULD YOU BE SO KIND AS TO DIRECT ME TO YOUR HEAD-QUARTERS, PLEASE?

THIRD ON THE LEFT, AND PLEASE DON'T HIT ME ANY MORE!

THERE ARE TIMES WHEN IT PAYS TO BE POLITE, OBELIX...

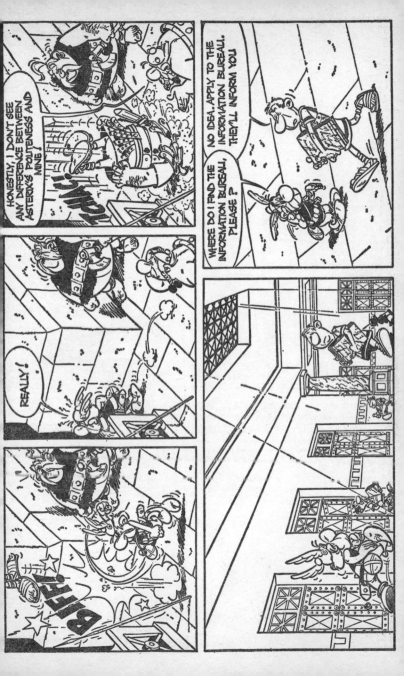

AH, HERE WE ARE...TRAGICOMIX HAS LEFT WITH A CONVOY. AT THIS MOMENT HE'S DUE TO TAKE SHIP AT MASSILIA WITH REINFORCEMENTS FOR CAESAR. THEY'RE OFF TO AFRICA.

TRAGICOMIX...WITH A "T", AS IN TIMEO DANAOS ET DONA FERENTES?

TRAGICOMIX

I'M RIGHT IN THE MIDDLE OF CARVING OUT THE LIST OF VOLUNTEER RECRUITS TO BE ISSUED TO ALL DEPARTMENTS...THERE HAVE TO BE TWELVE COPIES, WHAT WAS THE NAME AGAIN?

YES!

IS THAT YOU, ASTERIX?

OBELIX! COME HERE!

AFRICA... HMMM...

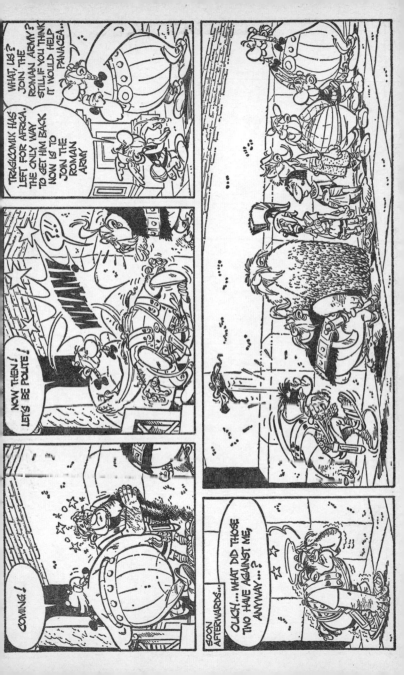

TERRIBLY SORRY

BAFFF!

CAN I BE POLITE TO HIM, ASTERIX?

GO RIGHT AHEAD, OBELIX!

YOU GET OUT, OR I'LL HAVE YOU IN THE COOLER!

RIGHT! YOU'D BETTER GO TO MARKET TO BUY WILD BOAR AND FLOUR AND EGGS AND SUGAR AND CRYSTALLIZED FRUITS. BEFORE YOU GO, PUT OUT THE FIRE UNDER MY CAULDRON

HAVE THEY GONE?

YES

NOW, ROMAN, LISTEN TO ME! ANY TIME WE'RE NOT SATISFIED WITH OUR FOOD WE'LL BE PAYING YOU ANOTHER VISIT! COME ON OBELIX!

SPLOSH!

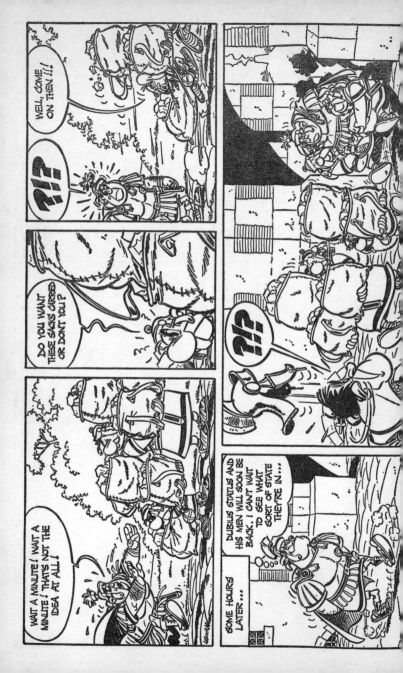